DINOFOURS™

I'M HAVING A BAD DAY!

For Anna and Maribeth Whitehouse
—S.M.

Text copyright © 1998 by Scholastic Inc.
Illustrations copyright © 1998 by Hans Wilhelm, Inc.
All rights reserved. Published by Scholastic Inc.
SCHOLASTIC, CARTWHEEL BOOKS and the CARTWHEEL BOOKS logo
are trademarks and/or registered trademarks of Scholastic Inc.

Library of Congress Cataloging-in-Publication Data
Metzger, Steve.
    I'm having a bad day! / by Steve Metzger; illustrated by Hans Wilhelm.
        p.   cm. — (Dinofours)
    "Cartwheel books."
    Summary: Tracy's day gets off to a bad start and keeps getting worse until her preschool friends show her how much they care about her.
        ISBN 0-590-03551-7
        [1. —Mood (Psychology) — Fiction.   2. Friendship — Fiction.   3. Nursery schools — Fiction.
    4. Schools — Fiction.   5. Dinosaurs — Fiction.]
    I. Wilhelm, Hans, 1945-   ill.   II. Title.   III. Series: Metzger, Steve. Dinofours.
    PZ7.M56775Dd   1998
    [E]—dc21   98-9301
                                                                                                        CIP
                                                                                                        AC

12 11 10 9 8 7 6 5 4 3 2 1   8 9/9 0/0 01 02 03
                                    Printed in the U.S.A.   24
                              First printing, November 1998

DINOFOURS™
I'M HAVING A BAD DAY!

by Steve Metzger
Illustrated by Hans Wilhelm

Cartwheel
·B·O·O·K·S·®

SCHOLASTIC INC.
New York   Toronto   London   Auckland   Sydney

A loud sound woke Tracy.

"Tracy!" yelled her big sister, Denise. "Don't leave your silly doll on the floor. I almost tripped over it."

"All right," Tracy said in a sleepy voice. "I won't."

Tracy slowly got out of bed.

"Tracy!" her mother called. "Please hurry and get ready for school. I have an early meeting."

"All right," Tracy said. "I will."

Tracy quickly ate breakfast and brushed her teeth. She didn't like having to move so fast, especially after her sister yelled at her.

"Let's go," said Tracy's mother, standing by the front door. "Good-bye, Denise. Don't miss your school bus!"

"I won't," said Denise. "Good-bye, Mom."

Denise didn't say "Good-bye" to me, thought Tracy as she walked outside. *I guess she's still mad.*

It had rained the night before, and puddles were on the ground.
"Wow!" Tracy shouted. "Look at all these puddles!"
She jumped into one and made a big splash!

"Now, look what you've done!" Tracy's mother said. "My papers are all wet! I'm very upset."

Tracy lowered her head and sang this song to herself:

My sister doesn't like me.
My mommy's very mad.
I wish that I were back in bed.
This day is very bad!

Tracy and her mother arrived at school.

"Hi, Mrs. Dee," said Tracy's mother.

"Hello," said Mrs. Dee. "That was quite a storm we had last night."

Turning to Tracy, her mother said, "I'm running late. I have to go. Good-bye." Tracy's mother gave her a short kiss on the top of her head. Then she quickly walked out.

She didn't give me my good-bye hug, thought Tracy. *This really is a bad day!*

Tracy slowly walked to the book corner. She found a book and sat down. As she looked at the pictures, Joshua came by.

"I love that book," Joshua said. "It's so funny. May I read it with you?"

"No!" Tracy said in a loud voice. "I want to read it by myself."
"Okay," Joshua replied, walking away. "You don't have to yell."

Later, Tracy decided to paint a picture at the easel. But Albert and Tara's fire truck was right in her way!

"Get this fire truck out of here!" Tracy shouted. "I almost tripped over it."

"Okay," said Albert moving it away from Tracy.

"What a grouch!" said Tara.

Tracy began to paint a rainy day picture with lots of clouds and puddles. She was just about to make dots for raindrops when her best friend, Danielle, came over.

"Hi, Tracy," Danielle said in a cheery voice. "May I paint with you?"

"No!" said Tracy. "You don't paint fast enough! You're too slow."

Danielle looked as if she might cry.

"You never said I was a slow painter before," said Danielle, walking away. "You're very mean!"

Just then, Mrs. Dee came by.

"Tracy," she said. "I think we need to talk."
Tracy looked up at Mrs. Dee.
"I heard you shout at Joshua, Tara, and Albert," said Mrs. Dee.
"And then you yelled at Danielle, your best friend. What's going on?"

Tracy's words tumbled out as she began to cry.

"My sister yelled at me because I left my doll on the floor," Tracy said. "Then, I had to move fast because my mommy was late. Then, Mommy yelled at me for making her papers wet. And she didn't even give me my good-bye hug."

"That's quite a morning," Mrs. Dee said. "It's no wonder you're so upset."

"Yes, Mrs. Dee," Tracy said, wiping her eyes. "I'm having a very bad day."

"Well," said Mrs. Dee, putting her arm around Tracy, "I hope you feel better soon."

"I don't think I will," said Tracy, returning to her painting.

Mrs. Dee quietly gathered the other children and told them what a bad day Tracy was having.

"How do you think we can help?" she asked.

"Let's make her a giant picture," said Albert.

"With lots of drawings of cars and trucks," yelled Brendan.

"We'll say all the things we like about Tracy," said Tara.

"And Mrs. Dee will write them down," added Joshua. "That will make Tracy feel better."

All the children shared their ideas. Except Danielle.

Mrs. Dee placed a large piece of paper with markers and crayons on the floor. Some children made drawings. Others asked Mrs. Dee to write down their words. But Danielle sat by herself at one of the art tables.

When the children were finished, Mrs. Dee taped the picture to the wall. They called Tracy over.

"What's this?" Tracy asked in a soft voice.

"We made it for you," said Brendan.

"We want you to feel better," added Tara.

Mrs. Dee read what the children had said and pointed out their drawings to Tracy.

"Thank you," Tracy said with a smile.

Afterward, Tracy noticed there was nothing from Danielle.

I was too mean to her, Tracy thought. *Maybe she doesn't like me anymore.*

Just then, Tracy felt a tap. She turned around and saw Danielle.

"I have something for you, Tracy," Danielle said. "I hope it makes you feel better."

Tracy looked at what Danielle had just given her. It was a collage made from bows, ribbons, cutout paper hearts, buttons, and pieces of fabric. On the bottom, Danielle wrote, "Tracy, I love you! Danielle."

Tracy grinned from ear to ear as she gave Danielle a big hug.
Then, Tracy sang a new song:

It was such a bad day,
I cried and had no fun.
But now my friends have made me smile,
A good day has begun.